A Time Travel Guide to the Future

Written by Isabel Thomas

Contents

Introduction

History tells us that the world in 40, 50 or 60 years' time will look very different from today. To find out how different, you need the ultimate futuristic invention: time travel.

Imagine that you can fast-forward to the future. What will the world be like when you're an adult? Will you wear spray-on clothes and take a floating train to work? Will your children log on to school from their bedrooms? Will your grandchildren play with robotic pets? Set your time machine to the 2050s and hold on tight! This is your guide to life in the future.

Why the future matters

Looking into the future is useful as well as fun. Governments and businesses want to find out what will happen in decades to come. They need to plan solutions to the challenges the world will face, such as climate change and growing populations, so they ask futurologists for help. These are scientists and other experts who study the world around us in order to predict what will happen in the future.

Progress so far: predicting the future

Humans have always been fascinated by the future. They have used many different ways to try and find out what will happen next.

Tea leaves

For thousands of years, people have looked at the patterns tea leaves make in the bottom of a cup. The shapes are supposed to hold clues to the future.

Astrology

Astrologers believe the future can be predicted by looking at the position of stars and planets in the night sky. Astrology is still used today to write **horoscopes**.

Weather forecasting

Scientists can use their knowledge of how the world works to predict certain things, such as the weather.

WEEKEND FORECAST

SAT   SUN

Welcome to the future

From your hotel room to the streets outside, be prepared for some big changes.

Helpful hotel rooms

You might not be able to spot the ultra-tiny computers in your hotel room, but they will spot you. As you use the room, every object collects and shares information about you using **wireless** connections. For example, your fridge tells your toothbrush when you eat something sugary, so that your toothbrush beeps and reminds you to brush your teeth!

Future fact file: computers

Advances in technology mean that **computer chips** are a thousand times more powerful than they were in the early 21st century. They're also smaller and cheaper, and this is changing the way they're used – increasing demand for computers that are even smaller, even cheaper and even more powerful.

Recycling bins send a message to housekeeping when they need emptying.

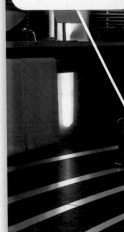

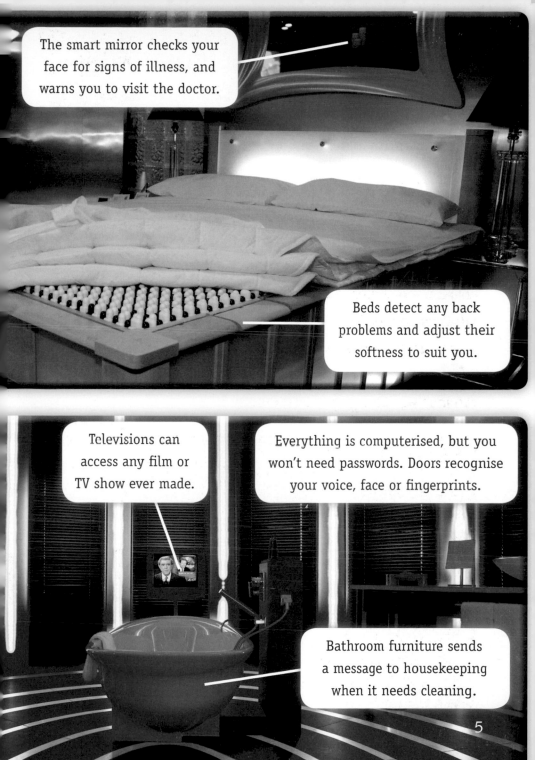

Hit the streets

Now that your hotel room has got to know you, it's time to step outside and take a look at the future. You'll notice that the streets look very crowded. The world's population has passed the nine billion mark.

Architects are designing taller and taller skyscrapers to house the growing population.

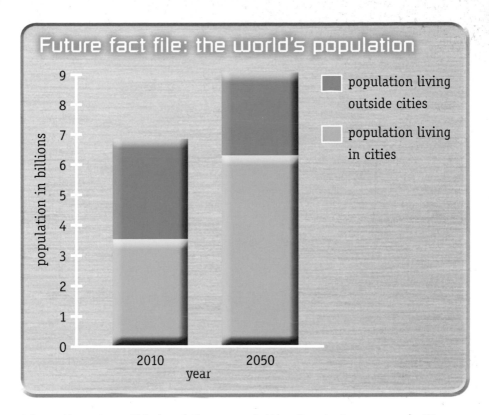

Future fact file: the world's population

- population living outside cities
- population living in cities

y-axis: population in billions (0–9)

x-axis: year — 2010, 2050

More than two thirds of the population live in towns and cities. Huge, sprawling "megacities" face a lot of challenges, such as providing food and clean water for everyone. However, they're also some of the most exciting places on Earth.

Ageing populations

People are living longer, so there's a high proportion of older people in the population. Back in the early 21st century, just seven in every 100 people were over 65. In 2050, the figure has risen to 16 in every 100. It's a big challenge to provide healthcare and pensions for all these elderly people.

Cashless future

There's so much to see and do in the future, but before you start you'll need some spending money. There's no need to visit a cash machine. Electronic money has taken the place of coins and notes. You can choose to store your digital cash on a smart card, or a gadget such as a mobile phone. Computers now need to scan the iris on your eye or recognise your voice to authorise a payment, rather than needing a PIN number. If you're going to stay in the future for a while, you might even get a payment implant – a tiny computer chip in your jaw or arm.

When it's time to pay for something, the shop's computers use wireless connections to "talk" to your payment device, and money is subtracted from your balance. Computer chips in vehicles automatically pay for petrol, tolls and parking, and people can even send you birthday money via text message.

New technology makes payment extremely fast. Every time you pay digitally, the bank records what you bought, where you bought it, when you bought it, and how much you paid. Because spending is easy to trace, no one can avoid paying tax. E-money has also reduced violent crimes like mugging. However, there is more cyber crime as criminals work out ways to access and spend digital money twice.

Progress so far: money

Objects are no longer used to represent money. Shopkeepers of the future would find a £1 coin as weird as a cowrie shell.

Cowrie shells

Cowrie shells were used as money by ancient Chinese and African people.

Paper money

Paper money was invented in China around 1,000 years ago.

Credit cards

Credit cards were introduced in the 1950s. They allowed people to pay for things without having to use coins or banknotes, by transferring money directly between bank accounts.

Chips

In the 2000s, Japan and South Korea introduced national systems for paying with mobile phones. In 2010, a Spanish beach club let members have small chips implanted in their arms to pay for drinks without having to carry money.

Getting around

In 2050, city centres are car-free zones. Banning cars means that people spend less time sitting in traffic jams. New and improved public transport systems will carry you into town. These trams, trains and buses use less energy per person and don't pollute city air.

No cars are allowed in the centre of Amsterdam. The best way to get around is on foot, by bicycle or by tram.

Places with good cycling networks, such as Vienna and Cologne, were the first to ban cars in certain neighbourhoods.

Some cities provide bicycles you can hire for the day.

Specially designed pedestrian zones make walking and cycling popular. If you need to travel several kilometres or get somewhere in a hurry, try an electric vehicle such as a Segway. These are speedy personal transporters that carry one person standing upright. They fit inside buildings, are easy to park and run on rechargeable batteries. You won't have to buy one: just pick up a Segway from any community rack, and drop it off when you've made your journey.

To steer a Segway, simply lean in the direction you want to go.

Fuelling the future

Outside cities, cars still rule the roads. In fact there are more car-users than ever, because the world's population has grown. India and China's enormous populations now rely on cars as much as people in Europe and the USA do.

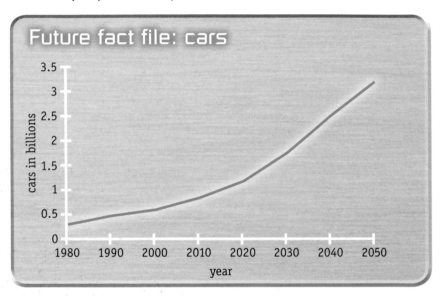

Future fact file: cars

The number of cars has tripled since the 2010s, and 80% of the new cars are in countries that are developing fast, such as India and China.

The world's oil supplies began to decrease in 2020. There is still oil in 2050, but it's much harder to get to and much more expensive. New cars no longer have engines that run on petrol or diesel. Cars in the future have electric engines that are powered by rechargeable batteries, solar panels or hydrogen.

Battery-powered cars

Electric cars were invented way back in the 1830s, but people preferred engines powered by petrol or diesel because they were cheaper and more powerful. Electric engines have now caught up. Over half of all cars in 2050 have electric engines that run on giant batteries. Drivers never need to visit a filling station – they just plug the car into an electric socket overnight. Electric cars use energy more efficiently than petrol and diesel cars, and don't release polluting exhaust fumes. However, these cars are only **green** if the electricity comes from clean sources, such as wind farms or solar power.

Cars of the future are small and light, so they use less energy and fuel. This electric car is having its battery charged.

13

Solar-powered cars

Solar panels change energy from sunlight into electricity. Solar vehicles use this electricity to power an electric engine. This makes them very cheap to run, because sunlight is free. However, solar cars are expensive to make and buy because solar panels are made from silicon. This is the material used to make computer chips, and demand has never been higher. Solar energy cannot be stored, so these vehicles are also unreliable on cloudy days and do not work at night.

Solar cars are most popular in very sunny countries near the Equator.

Hydrogen-powered cars

Hydrogen cars have electric engines powered by fuel cells.
Fuel cells turn energy from hydrogen into electricity, which
powers the engine.

a hydrogen car

Fuel cells are very efficient, and the only waste product is water,
which is clean enough to drink! Energy is needed to make
the hydrogen fuel, but as long as this comes from clean,
sustainable sources, such as solar or wind power, hydrogen can
be a very green fuel. Unfortunately these fuel cells are expensive
to make and there aren't many hydrogen filling stations yet!

Future firsts

Iceland's capital Reykjavik was the first city to switch
to hydrogen-powered transport. Its first hydrogen
buses were introduced in the 2000s. The country has
hydro and **geothermal** power that can be used to
make hydrogen in a clean, sustainable way.

Clever cars

Once you've chosen your car, you need to learn how to drive it. This is not as hard as it used to be. Every future car has a powerful computer built in, and computer chips are also found in roads, signs, parking meters and traffic lights. Their job is to make driving easier, safer and more fun.

As soon as you switch the car on, the on-board computer downloads traffic information from the computers in every road and uses it to plan the best route for your journey. Your car's computer communicates with car parks to guide you straight to an empty space. It warns you so you can avoid a crash with other cars.

Top-of-the-range vehicles can even drive themselves. Like autopilot on aeroplanes, the technology reduces human error.

This driverless car can carry four people at speeds of up to 40 kilometres an hour.

On long journeys, drivers can let the computer watch the road while they watch a film, eat lunch or get some work done. Computers don't get tired, meaning no more accidents are caused by drivers falling asleep.

Future firsts

In 2007 the first road race for cars that can drive themselves was held in California. Teams entered cars that had to navigate the city streets without human help. The self-driving cars of the 2050s are based on these early designs.

Long distance travel

In 2050, long distance rail travel is so fast that it may be quicker to go for lunch in another country than at a restaurant on the other side of your city.

High-speed rail

High-speed trains are powered by electricity from **renewable resources** and can reach a top speed of 480 kilometres per hour. A big advantage is that they use a third of the energy that aircraft use and produce no polluting exhaust fumes. However, high-speed railways are very expensive to build and destroy large areas of countryside.

a maglev train in Shanghai, China

Maglev trains

Maglev trains are powered by giant **electromagnets** and can reach a top speed of 400 kilometres per hour. The large magnets make the train hover above the track, so there is no **friction** between the train and track. This allows maglev trains to travel quickly without using as much energy as normal railways. But maglev railways are also extremely expensive to build so they are not available in many places.

Superjumbos

High-speed planes make it possible to take a day trip to the other side of the world.

Superjumbos are powered by liquid fuels made from oil or plants and can travel at 900 kilometres per hour. One big advantage is that fewer flights are needed because up to 900 passengers can be carried on each journey. This means that less energy is used per passenger. However, tickets are very expensive because most aeroplanes still use liquid fuels made from oil, which is extremely expensive.

In 2050 airline passengers travel in a much more comfortable space.

Hypersonic jets

Hypersonic jets can travel at an incredible 5,400 kilometres per hour, powered by liquid hydrogen. A specially shaped engine squeezes air from the atmosphere to help burn the fuel. This means that a hypersonic jet does not have to carry extra oxygen onboard, making it lighter and faster. It can fly 300 passengers from Europe to Australia in less than five hours. But these aircraft have a bad effect on the environment because they fly higher than superjumbos, and release water vapour into the **stratosphere**. This contributes to climate change.

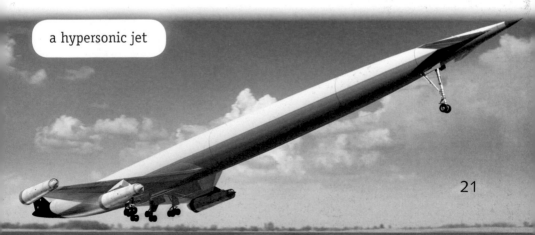

a hypersonic jet

21

Entertainment

Throughout human history, leaps in technology have made it easier, faster and cheaper to get essential tasks done. This means people in the future have more free time than ever before. They fill it with a mind-boggling variety of entertainment, including interactive television.

Channel You

Every television in the future is connected to the internet. Televisions quickly learn what you like to watch and then personalise every programme and advertisement. You can also interact with what you're watching. Films, dramas and soap operas are played as games, where the audience votes to decide what characters will do next. You can even upload your own videos on to thousands of specialist channels, and be paid by anyone who watches them.

In the future, you no longer need to wear clunky glasses to watch 3D television. **Holographic** displays create moving 3D images using laser beams. They are very realistic and can be watched from different angles, making television programmes and video games very exciting.

Future firsts

British photographer William Friese Greene invented a process for making 3D films in the 1890s. Two films taken from different angles were shown side by side on a screen. When people viewed the screen through special glasses, their brains were tricked into seeing a single, 3D image.

Future toys

If you're looking for a souvenir from the future, how about one of the amazing toys your grandchildren will one day play with? Toy inventors have used the future's new materials to create skateboards that can climb walls, full-size football goals that roll up into your bag and water pistols filled with "dry liquid". This liquid does get you wet, but it evaporates so quickly that you are dry again within seconds.

You won't stay wet for long in water fights of the future.

Future materials

When there was plenty of oil, plastic was the material of choice for toy makers. It's cheap, colourful and can be formed into all sorts of shapes. It's also robust and doesn't dissolve when chewed or left in the rain. But because the world's oil supplies began to run out in 2020, it's too expensive to make new plastic from oil. Manufacturers have found alternatives.

Recycled plastics

The landfill sites of the late 20th and early 21st century have become enormous mines. Rubbish is dug up and sorted to find valuable plastic that can be recycled. However, not all types of plastic can be recycled.

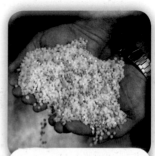

Plastic is recycled as many times as possible, but the quality gets worse every time.

Bioplastics

Bioplastics are made from plants that can be regrown. The downside is that these if these plastics get wet or are left outdoors, they will break down after a few months.

New materials

Exciting new materials appear all the time. Scientists can design materials that have all the properties of plastic. However, they are more expensive than real plastics.

Robopets

The ultimate computer-powered toys are robotic pets. Advanced **artificial intelligence** lets digital dogs interact with people in a lifelike way. They learn to recognise their owner's face and even respond to different expressions.

Speech recognition and language software are built in, so owners can speak instructions and digital dogs can actually talk back in the owner's language!

Like real pets, robopets make people feel calm and happy. In crowded cities and towns robopets are popular because they don't have to be walked or let outside. They can keep people company in nursing homes and hospitals. Real pets are not allowed in these places because they might carry harmful germs and would be difficult to look after.

Choosing a robot for a pet also means that you are not limited to dogs, cats and guinea pigs. Why not choose a pet dinosaur or a dragon that really flies? Most importantly, robopets don't demand precious resources like water and food.

Progress so far: electronic pets

Robopets have been on the market since 1996. The main aim for owners of these early robopets was to look after them carefully to keep them alive. Later types could move their eyes, mouth and ears, and speak words in the user's own language. Now some robopets even have built-in cameras and **sensors** that allow them to move in a lifelike way.

These robopets have all been bestselling toys.

Back to school

Don't worry about falling behind at school as you time travel.
In the future, children keep up with schoolwork from anywhere
in the world. They also expect education to be as entertaining
as their free time. Many lessons are held in **virtual** classrooms,
where children can log on to be taught by "super teachers".
These highly trained professionals can teach thousands of pupils
at once through webcasts – lessons that are broadcast on
the internet. Computer-generated characters have replaced
some teachers. These characters are programmed so they can
answer questions and spot correct and incorrect answers.

Paper and pens are things of the past. Pupils work
on tablet PCs, while books and posters are made
from ePaper, a type of ultra-thin electronic display.
This helps to save the world's trees.

Virtual classrooms allow children and teachers to work at any time of day. These classrooms don't need heating and light, and there's no carbon-guzzling daily commute to school. However, face-to-face interaction is still important to make sure children work hard, learn about teamwork and make friends!

Virtual classrooms mean that everyone can share the best teachers, no matter where they live.

What to wear

In the future, even your clothes are intelligent. Many garments are made from the latest "smart fabrics".

Tiny wires can be woven into fabric so that your clothes conduct electricity. Fancy a pair of gloves that can help you open jars? Some fabrics can give people extra strength. Their fibres get smaller and more compact as electricity passes through them so they can work with your muscles to make you stronger.

Some smart fabrics can change energy from your movements into electricity. These lightweight fabrics were developed for soldiers' uniforms in the early 21st century, to avoid carrying heavy batteries in war zones. Now anyone can power electronic devices by walking around the room.

Clothes shopping

Shopping for clothes is very different in the future. Everyone can buy **customised** clothes, made to order with the help of body-scanning pods. You simply stand inside the pod while a computer takes a 3D scan of your body. In-store "sew-bots" then make the clothes to fit your body shape exactly.

30

New types of materials

Different clothes-making techniques meet different needs. Synthetic fibres can be melted down and used to form seamless garments out of one piece of fabric, perfect for sports gear and comfortable pyjamas. People working with chemicals or in hospitals can even wear spray-on clothes that are worn once and washed off.

Future firsts

The world's first spray-on clothes hit the shops in 2011. "Fabrican" liquid contains thousands of tiny fibres. The liquid evaporates when it is sprayed on to a surface, leaving behind the fibres, which then bind together. Natural or synthetic fibres can be used to create fabrics with different textures.

Wear your world

People can now wear all the technology they once carried.
The spread of smaller, cheaper computer chips means that music
players, digital wallets and **GPS technology** can be invisibly
incorporated in clothes. Computerised clothes are studded with
tiny sensors that can detect changes in the environment.
Vests monitor your temperature and send wireless signals to turn
the heating up or down. Collars detect stress hormones in your
sweat and release soothing perfume to calm you down.

In the future, one jacket does the job of all these objects and gadgets.

This technology is fun, but it can also save lives. Elderly people can buy clothes that monitor their blood sugar, heart rate and breathing. Smart fabrics can be programmed to deliver medicine at the right time, put pressure on a bleeding wound, or call an ambulance if the wearer's heart or breathing stops. These clever clothes also monitor how dirty they are getting, and alert you when they need to be cleaned. There is no need to read the labels. The clothes give your washing machine instructions so nothing shrinks or loses colour.

Future firsts

In 2005, school uniforms with GPS technology sewn in became available in Japan. Parents used the technology to make sure children got to school safely.

Things to do

The future is packed with exciting things to see and do. You can travel the world from the comfort of your own home, or take a real trip into space!

Virtual tourism

Virtual-reality systems let you explore 3D digital maps of anywhere in the world, as if you were really there. Why not spend the morning in New York, go to Morocco for lunch, and watch the sun set in India?

As well as sights and sounds, special helmets deliver the smells, tastes and temperature of any destination you choose. Turn your computer on, plug in the helmet, and it's as if you can feel the sun on your face at a tropical beach, or smell street food cooking in a bustling town square.

Virtual reality prevents some of the bad effects of tourism, such as polluting air travel and damage to world-heritage sites. However, virtual tourism does not bring any money to the places that are being toured. People also like to meet face-to-face, so real tourism does still exist.

Future firsts

In 2009, UK mapmakers used lasers to create an incredible 3D map of the British coast. It was the first map that had all the details of a photograph, but also let people move around the picture as if they were really there.

Virtual-reality technology also lets you step back in time. You can eat with Egyptians, meet a Roman soldier or even have a lesson in a Victorian school. Putting on your virtual-reality helmet is like climbing inside a computer game, where everything looks, sounds and smells real. You can walk around the classroom, and hear the squeak of chalk on the blackboard. Your virtual-reality gloves allow you to write with an ink pen, or feel the beads of an abacus as you do sums. You can even speak to other children – but don't let the strict Victorian teachers catch you!

Future museums

People still like to see and touch historical objects in real life, and the best place to do this is in a museum.

You will recognise the artifacts in the early 21st century display. They include keys, which are no longer used. It's much easier and safer for doors, cars and safes to scan your fingerprint or eye. Newspapers, telephone directories and even posters have been replaced by speedy, interactive digital versions. In the future, even a computer mouse looks old-fashioned! Future children also think it's very strange that people used to push vacuum cleaners around rooms. Robotic cleaners now scavenge for dust as you get on with something more interesting.

You can also visit a library of books, listen to recordings and watch films in one of the 3,000 forgotten languages that died out between 2000 and 2050. Millions of stories, poems, songs and traditions have been lost, because no one can read or speak them.

Space tourism

Space travel is cheaper and easier in the future, so it tops any time-travelling tourist's must-do list. Why not fly to the edge of the atmosphere, and experience weightlessness? Or you might prefer a weekend break in an orbiting space hotel, for amazing views of our solar system.

Helium balloons that took you up to the stratosphere were exciting in the 2010s, but by 2050 tourism has gone much, much further.

Bounce, jump and soar

Best of all is a trip to one of the new moon bases. Gravity up there is just a sixth of Earth's gravity. Feeling weightlessness means you can take part in some amazing sports. Skateboarders and BMX riders can hang in the air for almost two and a half times as long as on Earth and perform incredible tricks.

Preparing for space holidays is more complicated than packing a suitcase and buying some sun cream. The two months of training includes trips in the "Vomit Comet". This aeroplane performs a special manoeuvre that lets passengers experience weightlessness for 20 seconds, so their bodies get used to it.

weightless passengers in the "Vomit Comet"

Future firsts

The International Space Station orbits Earth between 278 kilometres and 460 kilometres above Earth's surface. It was built as a research facility for scientists, but opened to paying guests in 2001. For £13 million, you could spend almost two weeks orbiting Earth at 28,000 kilometres per hour.

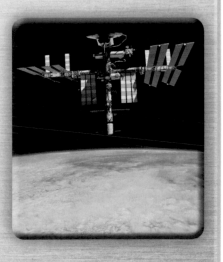

Space tourists can choose from a range of awe-inspiring options, depending on their budget.

Suborbital spaceflight

The Virgin Galactic SpaceShipTwo carries up to six passengers high enough to see the curve of the Earth's surface and experience weightlessness. A two-hour trip will cost you £200,000 and take you 110 kilometres away from Earth.

SpaceShipTwo's cabin

SpaceShipTwo (centre), attached to its carrier plane WhiteKnightTwo

Orbital space hotel

The Galactic Suite Space Resort has room for four guests and two astronaut pilots. Once in orbit it will circle the world every 80 minutes, giving tourists 15 chances to watch a sunset every day. Three nights away will cost £2.8 million and you will travel 451 kilometres away from Earth.

Luxury moon resort

The Bigelow Moon Base is made up of units that expand when they reach their destination, creating a comfortable environment for up to 18 space tourists. A six-month trip, taking you to stay near one of the Moon's poles, 384,000 kilometres away from Earth, will cost you £2.2 million per night.

the Bigelow Moon Base

Staying healthy

With Segways to dodge and space travel to master, you may pick up a few bumps and bruises on your tour of the future. What can you expect if you visit a doctor or dentist during your trip? Healthcare is better than ever, and people are living longer lives.

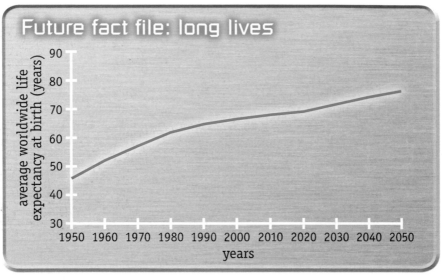

Future fact file: long lives

Robots at home

Computer technology allows sensors in your clothes or body to monitor your health at home. It alerts you – or your doctor – when something goes wrong. Tiny computer chips in the body can even release medicines when they are needed. This lets older people live in their own homes for longer. It would be too expensive to employ enough human carers to make daily home visits.

Robots at hospital

Machines have taken over many hospital roles, including cleaning, measuring out medicine and carrying people from place to place. Robots can even perform simple operations. They can make much more precise movements than humans, so they are perfect for tasks like making very tiny cuts.

Robots inside you!

Patients can be given robotic body parts that are controlled by a computer chip in the brain. Some people even choose to have healthy body parts replaced by robotic parts that do a better job, such as eyes that can zoom in to objects in the distance.

Future firsts

Scientists began testing remote-controlled robot surgery in the 2000s. The robots were designed to be operated from anywhere in the world. The best doctors could then carry out emergency operations on battlefields or in disaster zones, without getting into danger themselves and without delaying treatment by flying patients to hospital.

Predicting diseases

Doctors in the future can predict what diseases their patients might get before they fall ill. They use this information to prevent and cure many diseases.

A future doctor finds out what illnesses you are likely to get by studying your genes. These are instructions that tell each cell in your body how to grow and function. You have around 25,000 genes, which are a complete set of instructions for making you!

Everyone has a different mixture of genes, which are passed on from their parents. Certain genes make you more likely to suffer from certain diseases. Every new baby can have their genes analysed, to predict which diseases they might suffer from when they grow up. With advance warning, doctors can monitor the patient and treat diseases before they appear. However, some parents decide not to get their children tested. A person who knows they are likely to get a serious disease might feel sad and stressed as they grow up. They might feel pressure to save up for future treatments. They might find it difficult to get a job if employers find out they might need to take lots of time off sick in the future.

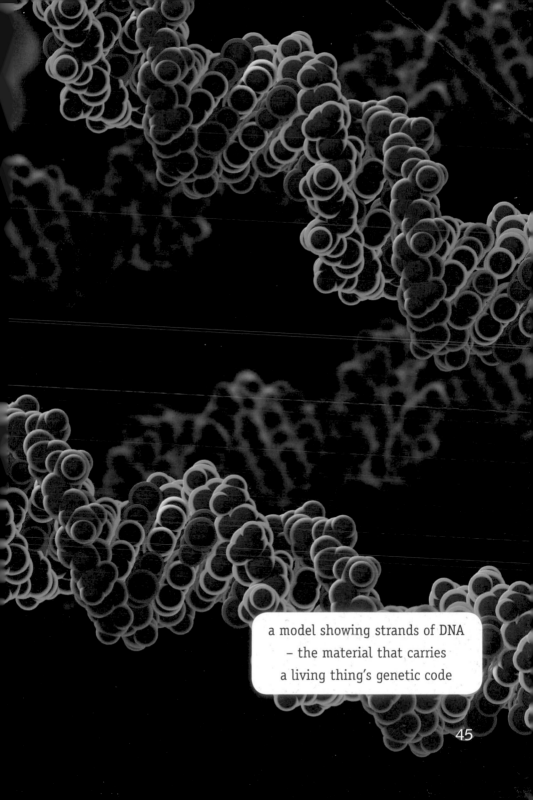

a model showing strands of DNA
– the material that carries
a living thing's genetic code

At the dentist

If you've forgotten to pack your toothbrush, you may end up visiting a future dentist. Look out for some strange new things.

The waiting room is full of babies

Babies don't have teeth to check, but they now have their gene

map checked at birth. Dentists can find out if they are among the three in ten people who are more likely to get gum disease when they get older. They can then give treatment to stop this happening.

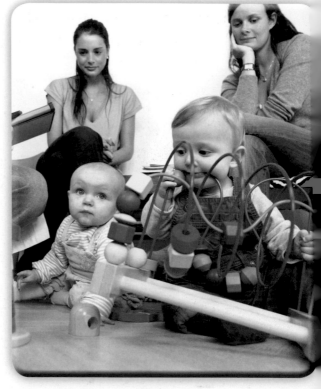

Dentists offer vaccinations

In the future there are new vaccinations against all sorts of things – even tooth decay. The vaccination helps a person's body to attack the bacteria that rot teeth. It is given to all one-year-olds, so that they never get holes in their teeth.

Dentists don't offer fillings!

You are too old to get the vaccination against tooth decay, but don't worry – in the future there is an alternative to drilling and filling. Scientists have found a way to grow new teeth to replace ones that are damaged or decayed. Dentists take special cells from deep inside your gums. They grow a new tooth in the lab and implant it in your jaw. Because it has been grown using your own cells, your body does not reject it.

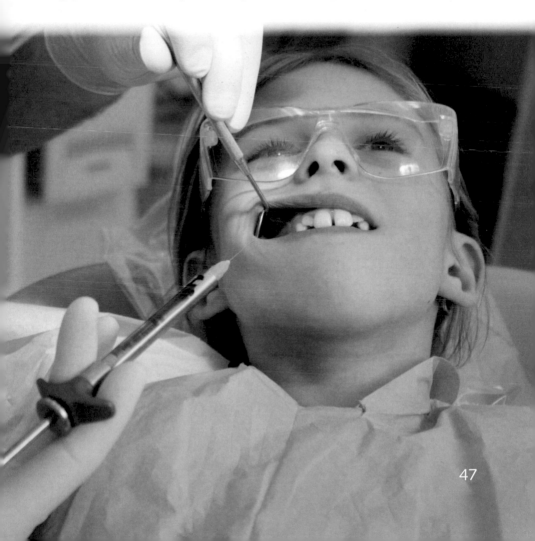

Climate and energy

Houses of the future are packed with new inventions, but
the strangest thing that you'll see is outside: the weather.
Your trip to the future will show you the effects of climate
change first hand. Back in your time, people are taking steps to
reduce the carbon dioxide **emissions** that cause global warming,
a rise in the average temperature of Earth's atmosphere.
It has taken many years, but the future world is gradually
changing the way it generates and uses energy.

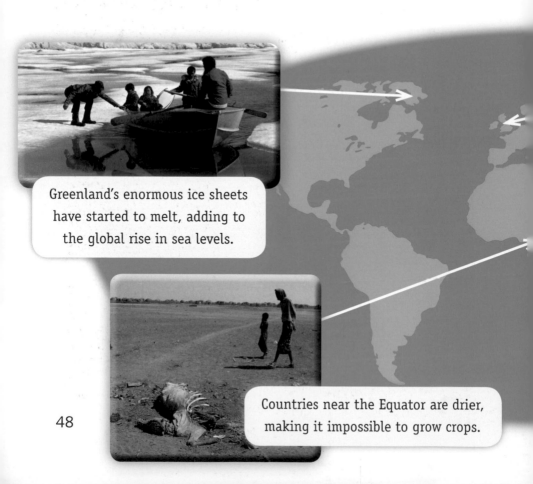

Greenland's enormous ice sheets
have started to melt, adding to
the global rise in sea levels.

Countries near the Equator are drier,
making it impossible to grow crops.

But global warming could only be slowed down, not stopped. In 2050, global temperatures are almost two degrees higher than they were before the **Industrial Revolution**. This does not sound much, but the effects have been huge. Water expands as it heats up, so sea levels have risen by almost half a metre. Heatwaves, extreme cold, flooding and tropical **cyclones** are widespread.

Countries near the poles have less rain in summer but much heavier rain in winter.

Flooding has forced hundreds of millions of people from the **deltas** of Asia to leave their homes.

49

Alternative energy sources

In 2050, the effects of climate change are front-page news every day. But people still need energy – and lots of it. There are more people, vehicles, homes and factories than ever before. The average amount of energy needed by each person has also increased, as living standards improve in developing countries. Energy in the future comes from a much wider range of sources, including renewable solar, wind and **nuclear power**. You are also just in time to watch the first trials of moon power.

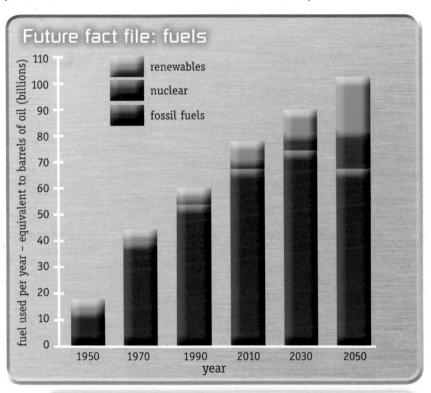

In 2050, fossil fuel use is falling, with a greater proportion of our energy coming from renewable sources.

a wind farm

Solar power from the Moon

Moon power is generated by solar panels on the Moon. These special panels soak up the Sun's energy and change it into microwaves – the type of energy that cooks your food in a microwave oven. These microwaves are beamed down to Earth, collected, and turned into electricity. They are expensive to make but unlike solar-powered cars that are only used by a few people at a time, these panels on the Moon can send electricity to millions of people on Earth.

In 2050, there are huge solar farms in deserts on Earth too, feeding power into the electricity grid – the network of cables that carries electricity across the countryside to our homes.

Solar panels work very well on the Moon because there are no clouds to block the Sun's rays.

How to be energy aware

In the future, using energy more efficiently is a way of life. Leaving the lights on in an empty room is considered **antisocial**. People are much more aware that small decisions about individual energy-use add up to huge effects. The energy-guzzling habits of the early 21st century are a thing of the past.

Even energy-saving light bulbs are old news. Future buildings are lit by **light emitting diodes** (LEDs).

These are the type of lightbulbs found on digital clocks and remote controls. The latest models are bright enough to light rooms and last for 25 years. They glow without getting hot, which means they don't waste energy as heat.

There are strict laws that make sure fridges, ovens and kettles use energy efficiently. Fridges even cut down food waste by monitoring everything inside and alerting you when something is about to go off. Everything from soap to shampoo is extremely concentrated, so that a tiny packet will last for months. This cuts down on the packaging and energy used to transport products to supermarkets.

Future fact file: the ozone layer

Chemicals called CFCs used to be found in every fridge and aerosol can. Many countries banned them in the 1990s, because they were damaging the ozone layer, the part of the atmosphere that protects Earth from the Sun's harmful rays. The ban worked, and the hole is due to close in 2068. This shows people that lots of small actions can affect the environment in a big way.

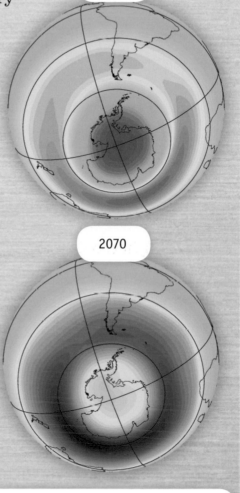

2005

2070

These pictures show the level of ozone above Antarctica in different years. Blue shows low levels of ozone, while red, yellow and green show higher levels.

Nature spotting

Sadly, future tourists are more likely to see animals in a virtual-reality experience than in the wild. Climate change hasn't just affected humans. It has damaged the habitats of many types of animals and plants.

Some types of animals have adapted by moving to different areas. For example, many mountain animals have moved uphill to get cooler. But flatter areas are so crowded with humans that most animals have nowhere to go. Towns, cities and farms have all expanded and natural habitats have been replaced with roads, crops and buildings.

The result is that the world has lost a million types of plants and animals since the early 21st century, including orang-utans, chimpanzees, dolphins and alligators. Millions more are under threat.

No more nature spotters

In the future, many of the wildlife-spotting trips that tourists used to enjoy are impossible. Warmer seas are killing coral reefs, putting an end to scuba diving. There are no safaris in the future because most big African mammals, such as rhinos and elephants, are extinct in the wild. Floods have destroyed many coastal habitats, and the animals and plants that lived there. Melting Arctic ice means that animals such as polar bears are dying out. Droughts and wildfires in dry areas have also wiped out many kinds of plants.

Protecting nature

People are fighting to save the plants and animals that are left. Every species is important to keep the delicate balance within its habitat. If one species is threatened then many others may also be in danger. Many threatened species are also important sources of food and raw materials for making things like medicines. Others may have amazing uses that haven't been discovered yet. This happened with the rosy periwinkle. In the 1950s, scientists started investigating this plant's ability to treat diabetes. However, during their research they discovered it could also be used to treat two types of cancer. The rosy periwinkle was rescued from extinction and has saved thousands of lives.

rosy periwinkle

Countries carefully protect the variety of plants and animals that are left, just as they protect their other natural resources. Rainforests are some of the most heavily protected areas, because they are home to a great variety of plants and animals. Technology is used to monitor threats to endangered wildlife and catch environmental criminals.

The vast size of the Amazon and Congo rainforests once made it difficult to catch people who were illegally cutting down trees, but now space satellites are being used to tackle the problem. These satellites take photos showing exactly where the natural habitat has been disturbed. Police can then be sent to the right spot in time to catch the criminals.

Future fact file: extinction

A huge fall in the number of sharks living in the North Atlantic Ocean has wiped out shellfish at the bottom of the food chain. The sharks were killed for their valuable fins. When there were no sharks left to eat fish such as rays and skates, there were more rays and skates to eat shellfish. When one animal or plant disappears from a food chain, the whole **ecosystem** is affected.

Artificial conservation

In the future, zoos are the only places where you can see the amazing animals that once roamed the planet and are now extinct.

Some of the animals living in future zoos are the **descendants** of zoo animals of the past. Others have been born using **cloning** technology. They are exact copies of animals that once lived in the wild. Before these animals became extinct, some of their cells were collected and stored in cell banks. Scientists now clone new animals using these cells.

Decades of practice have made scientists so good at cloning, they can bring back species that became extinct long ago. This is your chance to pat a dodo, feed a mammoth, and photograph a sabre-tooth tiger.

Dodos died out in the 17th century, but cloning could bring them back.

Future firsts

The first threatened
animal to be
conserved by cloning
was a baby guar,
a type of wild cow.
Conservationists
were worried that
this species might
face extinction.

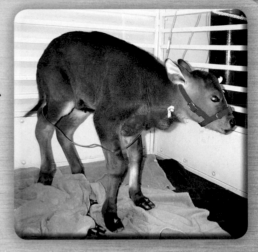

Scientists cloned the baby, called Noah, using
a frozen cell from an adult guar.

In the future, most people can only see wildlife
in virtual-reality experiences, or artificial,
enclosed environments like this one in Arizona.

Eating and drinking

As you spend more time in the future, you'll find out that food and water have become precious resources. Climate change has upset water supplies. Even future scientists can't make rivers flow and rain fall where they are most needed.

Water shortages

Enormous cities in Asia and Africa need more water than ever for drinking, washing, generating energy and watering crops. However, climate change means that many of these areas get less rain than they did in the past. Rivers and ground water are drying up. In 2050, 1.7 billion people live without enough water to satisfy basic human needs.

Searching for solutions

Technology is helping people all around the world to use water more efficiently. It has also given us new ways to clean dirty water so it can be reused. Some of the driest areas have gone a step further and are using clever new water sources.

Huge desalination plants that take the salt out of seawater are now as common as power plants in some parts of the world. Some heat seawater so the water evaporates while others filter seawater to remove the salt. Coastal countries will never run out of seawater. The downside is that desalination plants use lots of energy and won't work everywhere. You'll find them on the windy coasts of sunny countries, where renewable solar or wind energy can power them.

Future firsts

In the 1990s, a desert village in Chile was one of the first places to collect water from fog.

Collectors shaped like huge tennis nets harvested water droplets from heavy fog and fed them into pipes that supplied the village with 10,000 litres of water every day.

Feeling hungry?

Time travelling works up an appetite, but don't worry – future food doesn't come in freeze-dried, microwaveable cubes like science-fiction authors once imagined. Restaurants and supermarkets still sell the meals you're used to eating, but the way they're produced is very different. The pressure to feed more people while using less energy, land and water has caused big changes in agriculture.

Vertical farms

One exciting place to visit is a vertical farm. There's no need to pack your wellies, and no chance of driving a tractor. Vertical farms are skyscrapers where crops are stacked one above the other, towering up to 30 storeys into the air. This means they use 30 times less land than normal fields, and can be built where food is most needed – in the middle of cities. Crops are grown in water that constantly flows past their roots, delivering all the nutrients they need. Sensors monitor the conditions and send information back to a central computer that also controls the amount of light each plant receives.

This computer-controlled farming uses far less water and other resources than traditional farming, and produces almost no waste. However, vertical farms are very expensive to build so they are only a solution for wealthy cities.

Vertical farms are helping to feed city populations.

Creepy-crawly cuisine

Meat production has also changed. Farming large mammals such as sheep and cows uses more energy, land and water than any other type of food production. These animals eat crops that could feed humans, and they release gas that is a major cause of the greenhouse effect. As a result these animals are not farmed so much and there is a shortage of traditional meat.

Instead, how about grasshopper burgers or a handful of crispy fried wasps? In 2050, people in Europe and the USA are enjoying a source of meat that the rest of the world has been eating for thousands of years: insects. They are served up as sausages and hamburgers. They can even be dried and ground up to make flour for bread or tortilla chips. There are over 1,000 edible insects to choose from, but the most popular are:

- beetle **larvae**
- ants, bees and wasps
- grasshoppers and crickets
- caterpillars.

This meal includes a caterpillar, a spider and a cockroach.

Even scorpions are good for you.

Edible insects are packed with protein, vitamins and minerals. Some types, such as caterpillars, contain more protein and energy than beef or fish. Your body will get 430 kilocalories of energy from 100 grams of dried Sapelli caterpillars. The same amount of roast beef contains just 211 kilocalories.

Insects are also much cheaper to feed and harvest. Demand is now so high that many types are grown in managed forests, or among crops such as rice.

Futurology

At the moment, time travel is only possible in our minds.
There are no facts about the future because no one knows for
certain what will happen. Instead, futurologists, scientists and
other experts make "best guesses" or **estimates**. They use clues
from the past and present to work out what will happen next.

Lessons from the past

History tells us that the technologies we use today will become
better as time goes on. In 50 years, computers changed from
huge machines that filled a room into devices smaller than
a fingernail.

These 1960s computers filled
a room, but had less power
than the laptops of the 2010s.

Scientists predict that computers will continue to get smaller, cheaper and more powerful, until they are used almost everywhere. In the same way, experts look at how populations have grown and changed in the past to work out how many people will be living on our planet in the future.

What do people want?

Asking what people would like to do – or will *need* to do – gives big clues to what they will do in the future. Futurologists know that we will need to find solutions to certain problems, and this drives the development of technology.

What are scientists working on?

Most world-changing inventions and discoveries are not made overnight. Scientific progress builds on previous research in small steps. This means that scientists are already researching many of the technologies that will shape the future. Look out for science news on the internet or in newspapers to get a sneak preview of our future world.

Around the world, people are trying out amazing new things that will one day be part of everyday life. Families are living in sustainable homes that generate their own energy. Children are playing with exciting new hi-tech toys. Futurologists look for these little pieces of the future happening right now, and they predict which of these things will catch on.

Surprises in store

Every futurologist agrees that we should also expect
the unexpected. From penicillin to microwaves, there
are many accidental discoveries that have changed the world.
Perhaps you will discover the next big thing yourself!

Science and technology fairs like Singapore's Fushionopolis
give people a chance to try out the technology of the future,
such as this 3D head-mounted display.

Getting it right ... and wrong

All futurology predictions are estimates. Some will become reality; others may not. We know this by looking at predictions from the past.

It can be hard to tell which new inventions will catch on. When Alexander Graham Bell showed his first telephone to the American President he was told, "That's an amazing invention, but who would ever want to use one?" Fast-forward 100 years, and 1.3 billion telephones are being used around the world.

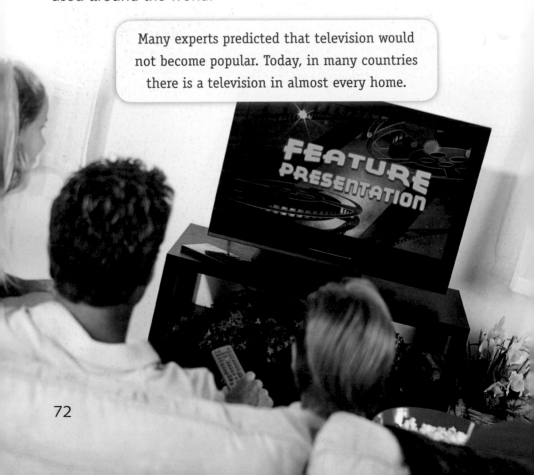

Many experts predicted that television would not become popular. Today, in many countries there is a television in almost every home.

Other inventions, such as floating cars, generated lots of excitement and then disappeared. In 1959, the car company Ford built a "Leva Car" that could glide on water or roads at up to 160 kilometres per hour. In the 1960s, the writer and futurologist Arthur C Clarke predicted that cars with wheels would be banned by the end of the 20th century. However, hovering cars never became popular because they would use huge amounts of energy, make lots of noise and fan dirt and water at pedestrians as they went past.

the Ford "Leva Car" from 1959

Designing the future

You will see the future yourself. It's not just today's scientists, inventors and politicians who will determine what the world will be like when you get there. You will help to shape the future too. Today's children will be the future's scientists, doctors and engineers. Maybe you'll be a future teacher, giving online lessons to children around the world, or a designer creating smart fashions or furniture.

All the products, gadgets and inventions we see around us started off in someone's imagination. Many of the wildest ideas of science fiction writers – such as satellites, space travel and eBooks – have become reality. One day, your imagination might help you to make a discovery or invention that changes the world.

Glossary

antisocial	harmful or annoying to the people around you
artificial intelligence	computer systems that can do similar tasks to a human brain, such as recognising spoken words, or making decisions
cloning	making an identical copy of something
computer chips	tiny objects made from silicon, with electronic circuits, which act as the "brain" of a computer
credit cards	a plastic card that allows a person to buy something, but pay for it at a later date
customised	changed to suit the needs of a particular person
cyclones	tropical storms where strong winds rotate
deltas	flat, triangular areas of land around the mouths of rivers; their rich soil means they make good farmland, but they are often vulnerable to flooding
descendants	people or animals that share a relative who lived in the past
ecosystem	a community of plants and animals, and their habitats
electromagnets	pieces of metal that become magnetic when electricity passes through a wire that is coiled around them
emissions	things that are produced and released
estimates	calculations or judgements about the future based on information that is available now
friction	the force that slows objects down when they slide against each other
geothermal	to do with or produced by the heat deep inside Earth
GPS technology	technology that uses the "Global Positioning System" of signals from satellites orbiting Earth to pinpoint where a person or object is

green	environmentally-friendly
holographic	producing three-dimensional pictures using laser beams
horoscopes	predictions about a person's future, based on the position of stars and planets
hydro	to do with water; hydro-electric power is electricity that is generated using moving water
Industrial Revolution	a period during the 18th and 19th centuries when new inventions led to the growth of mechanised industries, bringing about huge changes in the way ordinary people lived and worked
larvae	insects in an early stage of their lives, before they become adults
light emitting diodes	lamps made from a material that glows when electricity is passed across it
nuclear power	power generated by splitting the "nucleus", or core, of atoms, in reactions that release huge amounts of energy
renewable resources	sources of energy or other useful things, that will never run out
sensors	devices that allow machines to detect or measure properties of objects around them
stratosphere	the second layer of Earth's atmosphere, starting around 10 kilometres above the surface and finishing around 50 kilometres up
sustainable	able to meet human needs while also preserving the environment and natural resources
virtual	only existing on a computer
wireless	not connected by wires; wireless devices often use radio waves to communicate with each other

Index

We pay for everything with computer chips.

We interact with television programmes and upload our own videos.

We can eat, work or watch a film while our cars drive themselves.

We have robopets.

We learn in virtual classrooms wherever we are.

Our bodies are scanned so new clothes are made to fit us perfectly.

Virtual tourism takes us around the world without leaving our home.

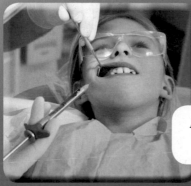

A vaccination stops our teeth from decaying.

Many more animals are extinct and habitats have been destroyed. These animals can only be seen in zoos and many have been cloned.

Insects are part of our normal diet.

Ideas for reading

Written by Clare Dowdall BA(Ed), MA(Ed)
Lecturer and Primary Literacy Consultant

Learning objectives: understand underlying themes, causes and points of view; use a range of oral techniques to present persuasive arguments; participate in whole-class debate using the conventions and language of debate; in non-narrative, establish, balance and maintain viewpoints; select words and language drawing on their knowledge of literary features and formal and informal writing

Curriculum links: Geography: What's in the news?

Interest words: climate change, futurologist, megacities, cyber crime, hydrogen, geothermal power, electromagnets, superjumbos, biofuels, stratosphere, holographic, artificial intelligence

Resources: internet, whiteboard

Getting started

This book can be read over two or more reading sessions.

- Look at the front cover and read the blurb together. Ask children to suggest what the photo might be of and what they think that the future might involve.

- Explain that this book predicts the future in 2050. Ask children to discuss how old they will be and what their lives will be like. List their ideas on a whiteboard. Establish that the book will make predictions based on current understandings, so the content is debatable.

Reading and responding

- Ask children to read to p21 silently. Explore their reactions to the notion of living in 2050 and ask them to describe which ideas they find the most surprising and why, e.g. the existence of more elderly people, living in a cashless society.